The Easter Egg Escapade

The Easter Egg Escapade

By John Michael Williams

Illustrated by Pamela R. Levy

Wonder Books
Boston
1993

For Karen, Jacqueline, and Alexandra, who are my
sweetest Escapade.
　　　　—J.M.W.

To my mother and my father, with love.
　　　　—P.R.L.

Text copyright © 1993 by John Michael Williams
Illustrations copyright © 1993 by Pamela R. Levy
Wonder Books, an imprint of Durgan Michaels Publishing
Boston, Massachusetts
All rights reserved. This book, or parts thereof,
may not be reproduced in any form without permission of the publisher.
To order, call (781) 245–3758

ISBN 1–883084–00–8
Library of Congress Catalog Card Number 92–083952

10 9 8 7 6 5 4 3

Third Printing 1999

Illustrations: Ink and watercolor on Winsor & Newton 90# cold press paper
Designer: Diane Levy
Text: 16/21.5 Goudy Old Style
Display: Adobe Caslon Open Face, set on Macintosh
Text Compositor: DEKR Corporation

Printed and bound in Canada

A special thanks to Duke University Medical Center.

Years ago, my sister Grace and I were going on a picnic and became lost in the woods. We were just small children at the time. Our wandering eventually brought us to Eggtown, which is the place where the story you are about to read happened. It was our good luck to be rescued by a cousin of Big Boring Benedict Bunny. He told us of an amazing escape while leading us home. As Grace and I grew older, we tried many times to find our way back to Eggtown—but we never again found the way.

—John Michael Williams

In his home by the brook near the top of a hill,
Benedict Bunny was sleeping until,
The sun on its hind legs stretched into the skies,
And the light from the new day shone into his eyes.
He realized at once as he buttered his toast,
That the chickens today would be meeting,
To carry the eggs from the Hatch House in Eggtown,
To color and sweeten for Easter Egg eating.
He thought of the noise and the time it involved,
And was starting to feel quite distressed.
Slowly he pulled on his trousers and shirt,
And buttoned his waistcoat and vest.
He then made his bed and washed out his plate,
And sighed as he walked out the door;
Big Boring Benedict Bunny was ready,
For whatever the day had in store.

He walked past the school house near Merrily Brook,
And glanced at the door to the room,
Where he taught the third level of Rabbiton reading,
And thought of the students with gloom.
This morning however, because it was Egg Day,
The school house had cancelled its classes,

· 4 ·

So Big Boring Benedict Bunny had packed,
Up a lunch of some toast and molasses,
To bring to the home of Miss Harriet Hare,
Who like Benedict dreaded the day,
Of the Easter Egg processing, mixing, and such,
And the noise of the young ones at play.

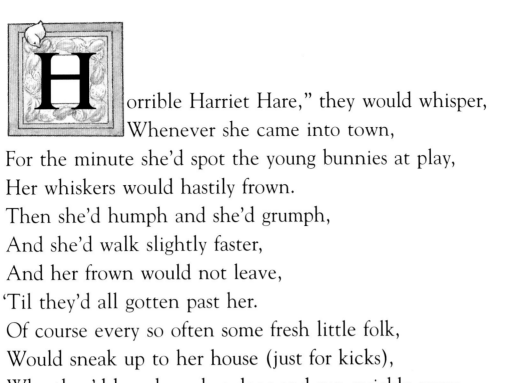

"Horrible Harriet Hare," they would whisper,
Whenever she came into town,
For the minute she'd spot the young bunnies at play,
Her whiskers would hastily frown.
Then she'd humph and she'd grumph,
And she'd walk slightly faster,
And her frown would not leave,
'Til they'd all gotten past her.
Of course every so often some fresh little folk,
Would sneak up to her house (just for kicks),
Why they'd knock on her door and run quickly away,
Or else chase her pet ferret with sticks.
Well she'd chase them away and they'd linger awhile,
As she hollered at them, "Beware!"
But the worst of it all was when everyone shouted,
"Horrible Harriet Hare."

Meanwhile in Eggtown excitement was spreading,
As eggs were placed into each crate,
And if not for the orders of Claralyne Cluck,
Why the trip would have started out late.
You might like to know (just in case you are asked)
That Miss Claralyne Cluck is the oldest
Of all of the chickens that live in the Hatch House,
And certainly one of the boldest.
In fact, once in a while you can still hear them tell,
Of the time that she chased off a Takit,*
Why Claralyne Cluck, she near pecked off his tail,
And told him that next time she'd break it.
And well you might ask, "Now a Takit: what's that?
Of Takits I never have heard. . ."

Well you might as well know that a Takit, indeed,
Is a lazy and thieving old bird.
They reside in the swamp under Merrily Brook,
And by birth they are chickens indeed,
But a Takit won't work; they would quite rather loaf,
And steal whatever they need.
Why one time in Autumn at quarter past eight,
Helen Hen had walked down to the water,
A Takit jumped out and the chase it was on,
But the Takit was faster and caught her.
To the swamp they did go. She was frightened, I'm sure,
To be caught by that slovenly bunch;
Why they would not release her until she agreed,
To go to the Hatch House and steal them some lunch!
Well of course she did not, but believe when I say,
She was frightened and chilled to the bone,
And ever since then it's a law in the town,
NO ONE'S ALLOWED (AFTER DARK) OUT ALONE!!!

*TAKIT: pronounced Take-it
Chickens by birth, gone astray, lazy, less attractive than most chickens due to their lack of grooming and work-ethic. Takits tend to live in caves and swamps where housekeeping is unnecessary. Originally spelled Takeit but changed by Benedict Bunny, schoolmaster, who felt strongly about Takits having three vowels in their name.

So the chickens arrived with their baskets of eggs,
And the greetings and such were exchanged,
The plans for the mixing and fixing discussed,
And shortly thereafter arranged.
There are bunnies and chickens to sweeten the eggs.
Helen Hen is in charge of the colors.
They paint and they polish and once in a while,
They stop for some tea and some crullers.
Helen Hen's job is just to be sure,
That eggs of all colors show up in the store.
So some will bake pink eggs with melon and cherry,
Add cinnamon sugar and lots of strawberry.
And blue eggs are special and so to be sure,
There are lots of blueberries by the Easter Egg Store.
And violets and lilacs with sweet cream and spice,
Make quite pretty blue eggs taste so very nice.
They have baskets for pink eggs and boxes for blues,
And bowls filled with sugars and honeys,

And every so often Miss Claralyne Cluck,
Will stop to shoo off some young bunnies,
Who sneak under tables when everyone's cooking,
And think there's a moment when no one is looking,
They fill up their pockets with chocolate and eggs
And run quickly away on their short little legs.

Not that anyone cares; there are plenty of sweets,
But a bunny or even a chick,
Might just eat too much and, well, nobody wants
Any young one to get sick.
So the day went along—it was hard work indeed,
And by night-time they'd finished the chore,
So they carried the eggs to the far side of town,
Where they locked them all up in the Easter Egg Store.

In the coldest and sloppiest part of the swamp,
Where the water is mushy and brown,
There's a dark, dingy tunnel which leads to the land,
Most often referred to as "Old Takit Town."

As it is all the bunnies and chickens alike,
Only in whispers will speak,
Of the dreadfully dismal and murky old town,
Where the Takits slither and sneak.
They were having a meeting in Old Takit Town,
And had just finished voting to steal,
All of the Easter Eggs locked in the store,
For their very next upcoming Easter Day meal.
The Takits were happy to take all the eggs,
They even believed it was funny,
That on Easter there wouldn't be colorful eggs,
Delivered to children from the Easter Bunny.
They finally agreed upon what they would bring,
And all of the things they would need,

And so "Terrible Timothy Takit"
   began,
His nastiest trip, his dirtiest deed.

"Terrible Timothy Takit,"
   you say,
Now why would they
   call him that name?
Well six years ago
   Eggtown's bake shop was robbed,
And he let his own mother
   take all of the blame.
Poor Tiny Tessie, why,
   all should have known,
You could easily give her a fright,
And when Tessie gets nervous
   or scared in the least,
She forgets how to talk
   and her lips will seal tight.
Her legs will start shaking,
   her eyelids will flap,
And the sight of it all is so odd,
For her beak twitches so
   that it forces her head,
To bounce up and down
   in a "yes" kind of nod.
Well the warm rainy night
   that the bake shop was robbed,
Timothy wore Tessie's shawl,
For disguise I am sure,
   and to also keep dry,
But later his mother
   was accused of it all.

Of course everyone knew just how much
    Tiny Tessie,
Loved plumcakes and pastries to eat,
And the very next day, why, the poor little dear,
Had just peacefully walked down the street.
When Boss Bunny Baker spotted the shawl,
And shouted at Tessie to stop,

And in front of
    some folk in the town
    there that day,
Accused her of
    robbing the bakery shop.
Well, a crowd gathered
    quickly and asked,
    "Is that so?"
Which then filled
    Tiny Tessie with fright,
And when Tessie got
    nervous or scared
    in the least,
She'd forget how
    to speak and her beak
    would seal tight.
They had quite a trial,
    and feeling so frightened,
Poor Tiny Tessie
    kept nodding her head,
Whenever they asked her if she was the one,
Who stole all the plumcake and cinnamon bread.
So of course when she nodded an answer of "YES,"
They locked her up in the jail;

And if you're caught stealing in Easter Eggtown,
They pluck half the feathers out of your tail!!!
All of this time, Terrible Timothy
Never owned up to his act,
While poor Tiny Tessie lost half her tail.

Believe it, this story's a fact!

It was only much later when everyone realized,
Timothy robbed the old bake shop that night,
And when Tessie got nervous or scared in the least,
She'd forget how to speak and her beak would seal tight.

But after this happened, poor Tiny Tessie,
Was never again the same,
So if you should see her you'll know it's because,
Timothy Takit let her take all the blame.
Now she's so nervous she hardly goes out,
And she totters around looking frail,
And to this very day poor Tiny Tessie,
Has only got half of her tail.

If you should venture near Eggtown some day,
You will notice as soon as you pass,
An extremely tall tree with a quite tiny house,
Overlooking a large field of grass.
And if you should spot it you'll say to yourself,
"That must be the world's tiniest house."
You'll wonder indeed if it's even too small,
For a bird or a frog or a mouse!
And you know, you'll be right, for you never would guess,
That inside that house, prim and proper,
Lives a fellow who's able to see miles around,
By the name of Good Gracious Grasshopper.
Who sits out on his porch with his sunglasses on,
Peering down over Eggtown below.
There is nothing Good Gracious Grasshopper won't see,
Nor something Good Gracious Grasshopper won't know.
He knows when the young ones are playing their games,
When the chickens are having a fight,

He heard Horrible Harriet scream at her cat,
When she meowed very loudly one night,
And when Claralyne Cluck saw a Takit one time,
And was chasing him off with a broom,
Good Gracious Grasshopper saw the whole thing,
With binoculars up in his room.
And then once in a while when his jelly bean jar,
Is beginning to get very low,
Good Gracious Grasshopper dons his best clothes,
And past Merrily Brook into town he does go.
And if you should see him be certain he will,
Be surrounded by townfolk all asking "What's new"?
And you'll hear him reply, "Good gracious, good gracious!
You all think that I have not much more to do,
Than eavesdrop and listen and spy on the town,
Believe me I never would snoop,
But good gracious! Good gracious!
Did you hear the noise?
Last Wednesday night at Miss Claralyne's coop?

And lately I've noticed that Harriet Hare,
And Big Booring Benedict Bunny,
Have lunch with each other quite often these days;
Together I find them quite funny.
Believe me I'm busy; no time on my hands,
To bother with gossipy news,
But good gracious, good gracious! I saw Helen Hen,
Walking her turtle and not wearing shoes."
This morning, however, Good Gracious indeed,
Set out on a quite different chore,
For he'd sp   ed the Takits with barrels last night,
Running away from the Easter Egg Store.
As he hopped down the street all the rumors began,
For Good Gracious was not even due,
To come into town for his jelly bean treats,
For another full week, maybe two!

So when he arrived at the center of town,
And nervously started to shout,
"Good gracious, good gracious, come bunnies and chickens,
Everyone, hurry! Come out!"
The excitement was spreading; the center of town,
Believe me was quickly soon filled,
For the thought of some gossip and a meeting that day,
Had everyone there feeling thrilled.
And when all had arrived, Good Gracious began
By saying, "I really would choose,
To not be the one to inform you all,
Of this dreadfully horrible news."
And with that not a sound could be heard all around,
As Good Gracious then said, "I deplore,
To tell you that last night I happened to see,
The Takits all leaving the Easter Egg Store!!!"

Well the smiles on their faces were gone very quickly,
And replaced with expressions somewhat more sickly.
Most of the young ones had started to cry,
Even Harriet Hare had a tear in her eye.
The ruckus and shouting went on for some time,
But everyone quieted down
When Miss Claralyne Cluck stepped up and began,
Speaking to all in the town.
"We have all lived in fear; we are chickens indeed,
Because of those Takits undaunted,
Who believe they can crawl to our Easter Egg Store,
And just steal all the yummies they wanted.
For years we've been frightened by that nasty lot;
I've seen young ones at night nearly shaking,
In fear of a Takit that might be around,
Just snooping for food for the taking.
I believe the time has now finally arrived;
Everyone's Easter was stolen last night.
We must go to the swamp and get back all the eggs,

Which are not even theirs but ours by right.
And," she continued, "I have an idea,
I have an idea that could work,
We can dress up like Takits and go to the swamp,
Where those lazy old creatures all lurk."
When the Takits start sleeping we'll tie up their legs,
And then we can all quickly pack up the eggs."
Big Booring Benedict Bunny stood up,
Facing everyone standing around,
And calmly announced he would head up a trip,
To the Takits' damp drizzly town.
"I am boring and careful and cautious," he said,
"But I live by the golden rule,
Which says bunnies and chickens and people sometimes,
Can solve problems AND still remain cool."
We can walk very softly, but quickly I'm sure.
We should all meet at twelve by the Easter Egg Store.
I'll make sure all goes calmly and hopefully then,
By mid-day tomorrow, we'll have eggs here again."

Then Harriet Hare,
    much to all their surprise,
Stood up and suggested
    the Takits' demise.
"I'll go with you also,
    and I will be cool,
For Harriet Hare
    has her own golden rule.
I will smack at their feathers
    and claw at their tails,
I'll make very good use
    of my long fingernails.
I will push them, and smush them,
    and whack with my broom.
They'll wish Harriet Hare never
    entered that room.
They'll lose feathers and rumpers,
    they won't sit for a week!
They'll have gums in their heads
    where there used to be beak!!
They will never again rob
    our Easter Egg land,
When they see what old
    Harriet Hare has got planned!!!"

Then she humphed and she grumphed,
And she walked slightly faster,
And her frown did not leave,
'Til a lengthy time after.

Then Good Gracious Grasshopper said, "I will go.
I am small, I'll not likely be spotted.
I can find where the Takits have hidden the eggs,
And help tie up the Takits as plotted.
The tunnel is dark under Merrily Brook,
I am sure they will never discover,
That I'm in the tunnel and snooping around,
For the eggs which we have to recover."

And then Helen Hen said, "Remember last fall?
When I went to the brook fairly late,
And a Takit jumped out and chased me until,
He caught me at quarter past eight?"
To the swamp we did go—I was frightened indeed,
To be caught by that slovenly bunch,
Why they would not release me until I agreed,
To go to the Hatch House and steal them some lunch!"
"Well of course I was saved, but I vowed one day,
They'd regret that they frightened me so,
I now know the way to that dreary old cave,
Which is why I will certainly go. . ."

But the biggest surprise and shock in the town,
Even more than the loss of the eggs,
Was when Terrible Timothy's mother stood up,
And offered to help save the eggs.
But poor Tiny Tessie, well, everyone knew,
You could easily give her a fright,
And when Tessie gets nervous or scared in the least,
She forgets how to talk and her beak will seal tight.
Plus her legs begin shaking, her eyelids start flapping,
The sight of it all is so odd,
Cause her beak twitches so that it forces her head,
To bounce up and down in a "YES" kind of nod.
But Tessie stood up and continued to speak,
While her beak twitched away and her legs became weak.

"Timothy Takit, my very own son,
Never owned up to the robbery he'd done.
He even allowed me to go to that jail.
He let his own mother lose half of her tail!
But when we reach that tunnel, and I reach my son,
Believe me he'll wish that he never had done,
The things he's been doing, like stealing our eggs,
TWO in this town will have wobbling legs!"

Right after Tessie finished her speech,
And the plans had been finally made,
They all rushed home to dress and pack,
For their very first Easter Egg Escapade. . .

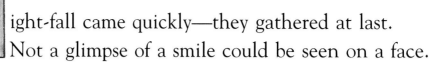ight-fall came quickly—they gathered at last.
Not a glimpse of a smile could be seen on a face.
All dressed up like Takits they quietly started,
Their trip to that frightening place.

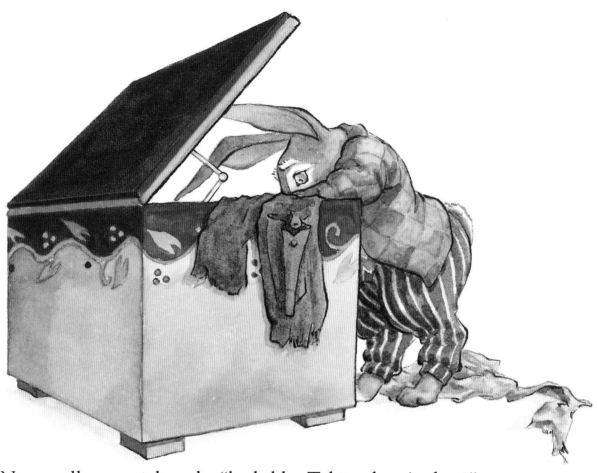

Now well you might ask, "look like Takits, how's that?"
Well a Takit will never be wearing a hat.
Their shirts must be soiled and wrinkled and ripped,
And the boots that they wear will not ever be zipped.
Their pants must be soggy and tattered and brown,
They will look like the very first pants made in town.
Their feathers are rumpled and shagged all amuss,
Clothing is not where a Takit will fuss.
But you'll notice the pockets on all of their pants,
Are quite long and deep just in case of a chance,
They discover a plum or a sweet that is baking,
That according to Takits is there for the Taking.

How the sounds in the woods made them shake as they walked,
And the scene was so eerie that none of them talked.
The wind off the swamp sent its Aprilish chills,
As our friends with their lanterns were treading the hills.
Even the crickets stopped singing their song,
As the Easter Egg Escapade travelled along.
And their lanterns, combined with the light of the moon,
Filled the trailways they travelled with shadows and gloom.

At long last they spotted a hole like a funnel,
(Which you can probably guess) is the mouth of the tunnel.
By this time our friends shared the one fearful thought—

Within any moment they all could be caught!

Good Gracious near shook like a leaf in the air,
But not any more than Miss Harriet Hare.

Benedict Bunny his face was near white,
Even Claralyne Cluck had now taken afright.
And poor Helen Hen, why the look in her eyes,
Was as if she had spotted a ghost in the skies.
(And of course Tiny Tessie kept fainting away,)
Not that any of them really wanted to stay.

But they all hunched together,
Like peas in a pod,
As each of them signaled,
Good Gracious a nod.
Our grasshopper friend thought his walk would not end,
As he entered the hall dark and spacious,
And the very last thing he muttered to them,
Was a frightened and whispered "Good Gracious!"

At the end of the tunnel right over the door,
Was a dusty and rusty old light,
Yet none of the Takits saw Good Gracious Grasshopper,
For he managed to stay out of sight,
As he crept past the entrance and into a hall,
He really was wishing he'd not come at all.
The Takits were there in the very next room,
And they truly looked scary in all of the gloom.

There were four in a corner at boards, throwing darts.
And two or three more that were munching on tarts.
Six at a table were lighting cigars,
With large wooden matches all painted with stars.
But just as our friend was near ending his walk,
As all of the Takits continued to talk,
The smoke from cigars and the tunnel's cold breeze,
Made Good Gracious Grasshopper suddenly sneeze.

And just one second later, to our friend's surprise,
He found himself blinking in Timothy's eyes!
And before he could move
    in a leap and a bound,
He was grabbed by a Takit:
    "WELL LOOK WHAT
    I'VE FOUND!"
And a frightened Good Gracious
    was held by his shirt,
As they grinned at each other
    and whispered, "Dessert."
"It's that snooping old codger
    from Merrily Brook.
Tomorrow for breakfast
    I think he shall cook."

"Some like them boiled or toasted with eggs,
Personally, I only care for the legs.
                    Yet stuffed is
                        quite pleasant and
                            mashed can be tasty."
                    While others believed
                        he would go well
                            with pastry.

"Though grasshopper sandwiches taste very nice.
But today, what with working, and really, the price,
Broiled with snakeroot
    and birch from the swamp.
I ask you: What more
    could a grasshopper want?"
"But better than that with some tea and some jelly,
Is a Good Gracious Grasshopper down in my belly. . ."
Then our poor little friend nearly started to cry,
As the cook for the Takits yelled, "Grasshopper Pie!"
He'd never been faced with this kind of ordeal.
IMAGINE IF YOU WERE SOME CREATURE'S NEXT MEAL!
And with that he was dropped in a rusty old pot.
Good Gracious Grasshopper really was caught.

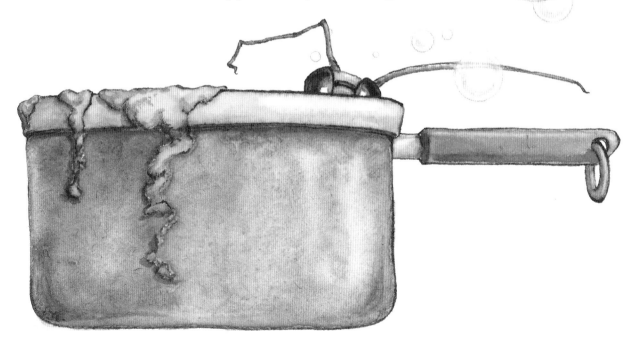

eanwhile, the rest of
Good Gracious's crew,
Were trying to figure out
what they would do.
By this time they realized
something went wrong.
Good Gracious Grasshopper
had stayed there too long.
They decided to enter
and finish the chore,
Yet it no longer mattered,
the Easter Egg Store.
They'd rescue Good Gracious
whatever the cost,
Even if all of their eggs
would be lost.

Eggs weren't important,
They all knew that now,
The question was really,
A question of how. . .

With a clang and a clap and a metal-harsh wham,
The cook pulled Good Gracious out of the pan.

"You must eat little one! You look so very sad,
And none of us here want you feeling so bad."
In fact you look hungry; have something to eat,
Why not a taste of an Easter Egg treat?
We are your friends; we are truly not bad,
In fact, when you came we were all very glad.
The swamp is so lonely, and more so at night,
We really did not mean to give you a fright,
A nice candy egg? I bet that makes you smile,
We're going to let you go home in a while.
It's just that you're tired and weary and…thin,
And you must be rested and…plump to begin,
Your long journey home, back to Easter Egg Land,
Have a bite of an egg dear,
    would that not be grand?"
You scared us, you know,
    when you suddenly sneezed,
But honest, we all are
    just so very pleased,
You came for a visit.
    That was terribly sweet.

"NOW WOULDN'T YOU
    LIKE TO HAVE
    SOMETHING TO EAT?"

Good Gracious Grasshopper
    looked into his eyes,
But all he could see,
    Were two Grasshopper pies. . .

"You are so very gracious," Good Gracious began,
"To offer me comforts in Old Takit Land.
 You're all much too generous and terribly sweet,
 To go to the trouble of having me eat.
 And I was not invited, you are only too kind,
 Yes, a morsel of egg I would really not mind.
 And seeing you have such a volume of eggs,
 One or two might be pleasant to, ahh. . . strengthen my legs?"

Good Gracious declared,
    "These are really quite tasty.
 Wait!!!" he then added,
    "I might be too hasty.
 My throat it is aching,
    and my legs they are shaking.
 What did they put in
    these eggs in the baking?
 What did they put in
    these eggs in the making?"

"I have pain in my back that
    goes down to my tummy.
What in the world? Why these
    eggs should be yummy.
Help me! Please! Takits!
    I'm dying, I fear,
The pain is much more
    than one fellow can bear!!!"

"What is this?"
    They've been poisoned!
These eggs aren't to eat!
And now I am sick, poisoned,
Grasshopper meat. . ."

And with that he fell down and just lay there so still,
While the cook yelled, "That grasshopper's dead!
Those eggs can't be eaten. They've tricked us I fear,
And put bad eggs for good eggs instead.

"Now what can we do? We've got nothing to eat,
  Unless you want sick, poisoned grasshopper meat.
  Yet that snooping old codger from Merrily Brook,
  Came to the swamp to steal back what we took."

"Which means they don't know something's wrong with the eggs,
  For they polished and packed them so nicely in crates.
  Let us go quickly. We'll hide in the swamp,
  Let them steal back all the eggs that they want!"

"And then when they eat them they'll die like their friend.
  That's our beginning, and that is their end.
  Then we'll take over in Easter Egg Land;
  We'll live at the bake shop; will that not be grand?
  We'll have all of their cooking and nice things to eat;
  We will never again have to work for a sweet.
  We must leave, hurry up! Don't bother with coats!
  Go now if we're going to pull off this hoax."

"Let them steal back,
  Their sweet Easter repast,
  For you and I know,
  This meal is their last!!!"

The Takits piled out by their soggy trap door,
As the rest of our friends came to finish their chore.
Claralyne shouted out, "Look what I've found!!!"
As little Good Gracious lay still on the ground,
All eyes filled with tears at the sight of their friend,
Who came in so bravely to meet with his end.
They lifted him gently up off the ground,
And stood for a moment, their heads bowing down.

"Good gracious!" Good Gracious said, "Friends, I am fine!
But Hurry, we really do not have much time!
We must get the eggs now before they come back.
Hurry! Let's hurry! Good gracious! Lets pack!!!"

As they ran from the swamp, our friend told his story,
He just could not wait to bask in the glory.
And proud? Well I think that he had every right,
For clever and brave was Good Gracious that night.

And the Takits soon heard what Good Gracious had done.
All the eggs were recovered; our heroes had won.
The Takits had nothing to eat except flies.
No sweet candy eggs, no grasshopper pies.

But in Easter Eggtown, the best Easter day meals!
The eggs and the parties, the little one's squeals,
The pride in the town both thankful and grand,
It was the best Easter ever in Easter Egg Land.

The End